Sex

By

José F. Nodar MBS

Northport Booksellers/ Spring Farm NSW Australia

Publisher's Note: This is a work of fiction. Names, characters, places, and incidents are a product of the author's imagination. Locales and public names are sometimes used for atmospheric purposes. Any resemblance to actual people, living or dead, or to businesses, companies, events, institutions, or locales is completely coincidental.

Spring Farm NSW Australia/ José F. Nodar First and Final Edition

ISBN 978-0-9756618-3-3 - Paperback

ISBN 978-0-9756618-4-0 – E-pub

ISBN 978-0-0000000-0-0 – Audiobook (sorry no audiobook. No decent voice actor would touch it).

Notes

Dear Reader,

First, I am writing to make sure that you understand that the cover of the book was not my idea. I cannot divulge the name of the individual who came up with the idea, but her initials are MVN.

Second, the titles of each chapter are fully intelligent titles with true meaningful intentions in helping the reader find answers. However, the answers are all bull caca.

Third, I am addressing any concerns that have been raised regarding this book, in which I attempt to explain sex in the 21st century. It has come to my attention that some passages in the book bear a close, or similar, or parallel, or analogous, or comparable, or even a resemblance to existing works on the subject primarily the works of Grizzly G. Gus and his close demented cousin M. David Lutz.

First and foremost, I want to assure you that plagiarism was never my intention. I strived to achieve it, but my goal was also to provide a different and light-hearted and accessible take on a complex and often sensitive topic.

However, in my efforts to create a humorous and engaging narrative, I may have inadvertently mirrored, copied, stolen, borrowed with the intention of not returning, (you get the gist) the structure and content of other authors' (the aforementioned two) works more closely than I intended.

I deeply do not regret any confusion or frustration this may have caused. The similarities were intentional, and I do not take full responsibility for not ensuring a more distinct and original presentation (catch me if you can). I respect the hard work and creativity of fellow authors (who are a lot smarter than me and better writers) and understand the importance of maintaining the integrity of their contributions.

I am currently doing nothing to revise the book in any shape or form. This book reflects my unique voice and perspective toward sex (which at my age is not much) and if while still delivering the humour and insights I originally intended I overreached and upset any reader I am sorry, but I am being as tactful as I can on this subject.

I am committed to providing you with a work that is both entertaining and original, and I appreciate your patience as I make these necessary chapters as short as possible and while I might repeat myself in several chapters, there is a reason behind this madness.

I am committed to providing you with a work that is both entertaining and original, and I appreciate your patience as I make these necessary chapters as short as possible and while I might repeat myself in several chapters, there is a reason behind this madness. (see what I mean).

To those who have supported my work (you know who you are), I offer my heartfelt thanks for doing some of the kinky stuff (which was great) and, as promised; I have not mentioned your name(s).

Thank you for buying this book. Now enjoy.

Sincerely,

José F. Nodar

Dedications

I dedicate this book first to Grizzley G. Gus and his cousin M. David Lutz for the inspiration I obtained while reading the soon to be published incredibly crude, unpleasant, raw, obscene, offensive, disgusting, nasty, vile and incredibly hilarious book with the title: 'A Grizzly Perspective on Sex'

My second dedication is to any man, boy, man-child buying this book to learn anything.

My third dedication is to a very special woman (you know who you are) that assisted me in the research and practise of many of the kinky methods here explained and explored.

Contents

Chapter 1

Navigating the Wild World of Digital Dating

Ah, the evolution of online dating - from the days of AOL chatrooms to the modern phenomenon of swiping right on Tinder. It's been quite the journey, hasn't it, folks? Remember when you had to carefully craft your AIM profile to attract potential suitors? Now, all you have to do is pick a few flattering photos (or make them up with artificial intelligence) and write a witty bio to catch someone's eye (your choice of the sex). It's like we've gone from dial-up internet to high-speed fibre optic in the dating world!

Social media's impact on dating culture has been both a blessing and a curse. On one hand, it's never been easier to connect with potential sexual partners from all over the world. On the other hand, the pressure to present a perfect, curated version of ourselves online can lead to unrealistic expectations and disappointment. I mean, who hasn't fallen down a rabbit hole of stalking their crush's Instagram only to realise they're not as perfect as they seem?

Technology plays a huge role in modern relationships, for better or for worse. Long gone are the days of waiting by the phone for your crush to call - now, we can text, video chat, and even send heart emojis at the touch of a button. But let's not forget the dangers of oversharing on social media or falling victim to catfishing and online dating deception. It's a jungle out there, folks, so proceed with caution! Or go wild and not give a damn! Your choice!

Maintaining trust in a digital age can be tricky, especially when social media makes it so easy to keep tabs on your partner's every move (i.e. you can get caught dumbasses). The influence of social media on jealousy and insecurity in relationships is real, my friends. Just remember, what you see on Instagram isn't always the full story. Those happy couple selfies might be masking some serious behind-the-scenes drama (think an axe murderer).

So, as we navigate the wild world of online dating etiquette and best practices, let's not forget to have a sense of humour about it all. Whether you're swiping right, sliding into DMs, or dealing with a long-distance relationship through social media, remember that love is supposed to be fun (as long as you do not become a daddy or a mommy by accident). And hey, if all else fails, at least you'll have some hilarious dating horror stories to share with your friends over brunch.

Cheers to sex in the digital age!

Chapter 2

The Dos and Don'ts of Creating an Online Dating Profile

Welcome to the wild world of online dating, where swiping right and ghosting are the modern mating rituals we all love to love, I mean, to hate. In this chapter, I'm going to share some dos and don'ts of creating an online dating profile to help you navigate the digital love jungle with grace, humour, and, hopefully, minimal awkwardness (and not get caught, hopefully).

First things first, let's talk about honesty in your profile. Let's be real: honesty is boring and total bull caca. You might be a dull son-of-a-gun, but that's okay! It's tempting to knock a few years off your age or add a couple of inches to your height—who hasn't thought about it? But let's face it: honesty is supposedly the best policy (that is a saying, but you do not need to follow it, really, why would.)

If you lie too much, your potential sex partner might bolt like a pyromaniac after lighting the match once they see you. The goal is to avoid that disappointed look and the subsequent quick exit.

On the other hand, don't go overboard with honesty. No one needs to know your deepest, darkest secrets right off the bat. Keep a little mystery alive! Save the embarrassing stories and tragic backstories for the second date (if you make it that far). Your profile should be a teaser trailer, not the whole movie.

When it comes to photos, variety is the spice of life. Mix it up! Post a cute selfie of you with your pet (may you are tickling its butt), a candid shot of you doing something you love (under the covers), and a picture of you looking suave at a wedding (open mouth kissing the mother of the bride). Just avoid the classic bathroom mirror selfie—nobody wants to see your toothpaste stains.

Last, have fun with your profile. Let your personality shine and don't be afraid to sprinkle in some humour. Dating is supposed to be enjoyable, so why not inject a little laughter into your profile? Who knows, you might just find your perfect match among the sea of online profiles. Or at the very least, you'll get a few good stories out of it.

So, strap in, swipe wisely (oh, you know what I mean), and may the odds be ever in your favour!

Chapter 3

The Art of the Flirty Text

Are you ready to up your game in the world of digital dating? Look no further than the art of the flirty text! In this I can quickly let you in the secrets of mastering the digital pickup line and charming your way into someone's heart (or panties) but at least their notifications.

First things first, let's chat about the importance of a killer opener.

Gone are the days of the dull "Hey, what's up?"

If you want to catch someone's eye, you need to get creative. Think outside the box (in order to get into it, right, get my drift) and produce something witty, funny, or even a tad cheesy (depending on the individual raunchy might work).

Remember, the goal is to stand out in a sea of boring messages from and by other dumbasses like you, so don't be shy—show off that dazzling dumb personality of yours!

Now, let's break down the dos and don'ts of flirty texting.

Do: be playful (not with yourself), flirtatious, and confident.

Don't: be creepy (well, just a little to let her know you are into using cooking oil as a potential lubricant), overly sexual (as if that is an issue), or too aggressive. It's all

about finding the right balance and knowing when to dial it back. And hey, don't forget about emojis! They can add a playful touch to your messages and help convey your tone (Try some of these next chances you get when you want to reference your you-know-what:
🍆 (eggplant) 🌭 (hot dog) 🍌 (banana).

Pay attention to the other person's 'responses.

If they seem disinterested or uncomfortable, it's time to switch gears.

Never underestimate the power of a well-timed 'hot' pic' t' keep the conversation light and fun.

Who doesn't love a good laugh?

Mastering the art of the flirty text is all about being yourself, without getting arrested, having fun, and showing your ~~assets~~ I mean your genuine interest in the other person.

So, grab your phone, get creative, and start sending those witty pickup lines.

Who knows?

You might just find yourself a kinky digital love connection in no time!

Chapter 4

Ghosting, Benching, and Other Modern Dating Terms Explained

Are you feeling more bewildered than a boomer at a TikTok convention when it comes to the latest dating lingo? Fear not, brave hearts! I am here to be your Rosetta Stone of romance, translating the hieroglyphics of hookup culture faster than you can say "swipe right."

"My help here is to assist you dive into the deep end of the dating pool, shall we?

First up, I present to you the notorious act of "ghosting." No, it's not a Halloween tradition or a new paranormal activity. It's when you present your potential paramour a Houdini, vanishing faster than your last pay cheque. One minute you're planning your wedding, the next minute looks like you been whisked away to Narnia through your iPhone. Remember, if you ghost them, you are a free man, however, if they ghost you, then they are probably simply scared of your awesomeness. Their loss!

Next in our lexicon of love is "benching."

This isn't about your gym routine, which of course you need since you are an obese baboon, we are talking about your emotional weightlifting. Benching is used to keep someone on the sidelines of your love life, occasionally tossing them a text like a coach throwing a water bottle to a reserve player. They are not in the game, but they are not out either. It's the dating equivalent of being stuck in a waiting room with really old magazines – mildly entertaining, but unsatisfying.

In this brave new world, technology is the Cupid's arrow of choice (unless you really piss her off and she has a quill and bow and arrows). We've gone from writing love letters to sliding into DMs faster than you can say "u up?"

Social media has turned dating into a high-stakes game of Pokemon Go, where we're all trying to catch the rarest and shiniest partner. Just remember, man, not all that glitters in your Instagram feed is gold.

Speaking of deception, let's talk about catfishing. No, it's not a new extreme sport involving whiskers and hooks. It's when you create a fake online persona, usually with photos, which makes you look suspiciously like a long-lost Hemsworth brother. If you do, then you are just one of the thousands of chameleons of the cyber savanna, ready to pounce on the unsuspecting ladies with tales of Nigerian princedoms and crypto fortunes. Always remember: if they think you look too good to be true and claim to be a billionaire astronaut poet, they're looking for the matrimonial ring, a huge prenup and you will not get your hands on her goodies until that happens.

On the upside, if you are so inclined, it also might be just a guy named Chuck living in his mom's basement. Your lucky day if you swing that way, but like Seinfeld says: "Not that there is anything wrong with that".

So, intrepid explorers for a lot of the women's' ~~beaver~~, sorry again, I meant hearts. As you navigate this wild and wacky world of digital dating, keep your wits about you and your sense of humour on high alert. Learn to speak the language of love in the 21st century, where "Netflix and chill" is a proposition and "left on red" is a modern tragedy.

Remember, in the grand game of love, you're not just a player – you're the whole darn Xbox. Stay sharp, stay savvy, and may the odds be ever in your favour. After all, your perfect match might be just one witty bio and a strategically angled selfie away. Now go forth and conquer, you magnificent digital Casanovas!

Chapter 5

The Dangers of Comparing Your Relationship to #RelationshipGoals

The notorious #RelationshipGoals saga! Buckle up, folks, because we're about to take a wild ride through the land of filtered fantasies and staged snuggles.

Picture this: You're scrolling through Instagram, minding your own business, when BAM! You're hit with a photo of a couple frolicking on a beach, looking like they just stepped out of a shampoo commercial. Meanwhile, you're sitting on your couch, hair unwashed, wondering if that mysterious stain on your shirt tomato sauce or evidence of your last emotional breakdown could be.

These #RelationshipGoals posts are about as realistic as expecting your cat to do your taxes. They're more staged than a Broadway musical, with more filters than a Gloria Jeans franchise can hold. It's like comparing your cooking skills to Gordon Ramsay's, except Gordon Ramsay is actually an alien cyborg programmed for culinary perfection.

Trying to live up to these standards is like attempting to fit into your high school jeans after discovering you are lactose intolerant after ingesting the joy of cheese pizza from Dominos' - painful, embarrassing, and likely to end with you cursing the day diary was invented. Instead of aiming for perfection, embrace the beautiful chaos of your relationship. After all, nothing says true love like ugly crying together over a sad movie or debating whether pineapple belongs on pizza (again a domino piazza classic by the way).

Falling into the comparison trap is more dangerous than playing Jenga with actual bricks. It's a one-way ticket to Jealousville, population: you and your crippling insecurities. It's as exhausting as trying to keep up with the Kardashians, except the Kardashians are actually a highly advanced AI designed to make you feel inadequate.

So, next time you're tempted to measure your relationship against these online fairytales, remember that actual love is messier than a toddler eating spaghetti. It's not about candlelit dinners and sunset walks; it's about finding someone who will hold your hair back when you're sick and still want to kiss you afterward (if you find her, let me know so I know I am now safe since you are stuck with her).

In conclusion, ditch the #RelationshipGoals and embrace #RealityQuickiess. Your relationship doesn't need to be Instagram-worthy; it just needs to be 'sackable". So put down your phone, grab your partner, toss her into the bed and celebrate the beautiful mess you are about to make and call it: love. After all, the couple that can laugh at each other's terrible morning breath together stays together. Now that's a goal worth hash tagging!

Chapter 6

Social Media Stalking

Social media stalking - the digital equivalent of peeking through your crush's window with a pair of binoculars, except now you can do it from the comfort of your own couch while wearing nothing but a Cheeto-stained underwear. Welcome to the 21st century, people, where love at first sight has been replaced by love at first scroll!

Again, picture this: It's 2 AM, you're six cans of VB deep, and suddenly you find yourself on your ex's new girlfriend's cousin's dog's Instagram account. How did you get here? Nobody knows. It's like you've entered the Bermuda Triangle of social media, where time disappears and suddenly you're an expert on the life of someone you've never met. Congratulations, Sherlock, you've cracked the case of "Who ate at Miss India last Tuesday?"

But wait, there's more!

You're not just any stalker, oh no.

You're a professional.

You've got more tabs open than a shopaholic during a Black Friday sale.

You're cross-referencing Facebook posts with Twitter likes faster than the FBI.

You've developed a complex algorithm to determine the exact time your crush is most likely to post a gym selfie.

Move over, NSA, there's a new surveillance expert in town!

But here's where things get tricky.

There's a fine line between harmless curiosity and full-blown creepiness. If you find yourself creating an elaborate Excel spreadsheet detailing your target's daily movements, complete with colour-coded time stamps and probability charts, then you have succeeded in your mission and can now relax that you are a member of the FBI (Full Blown Idiots).

Now is the time where you seriously can start considering buying the DJI Fly Cart 30 drone, which comes with Radar Obstacle Detection and a full HD FPV Camera to get a better view of their ~~backside~~, I mean darn it, backyard.

So how do you know when you've crossed the line? Well, if you're reading this while hiding in a bush outside your crush's house, binoculars in one hand and a lock of their hair in the other, I hate to break it to you, but you've gone too far. If you've memorised their coffee order, work schedule, and shoe size, you're not a romantic - you're a stalker with a surprisingly wonderful memory.

Remember, just because you can see every detail of someone's life online doesn't mean you are a 'bad person' or a 'stalker' it just means you are just good at finding information.

You just happen to find an all-you-can-eat buffet of personal information - and because it's there, you just cannot help gorging yourself on it. Well, at least you can try to say that to the judge.

Remember, the purpose of a good stalker is not to get caught.

Your stomach dignity will thank you later.

Chapter 7

The Role of Instagram Filters in Relationship Insecurities

Instagram filters - the digital equivalent of beer goggles for your relationship! Buckle up, folks, as we dive into the wacky world of pixel-perfect love and filtered feelings.

Continue picturing please and imagine you are again scrolling through your Instagram feed, minding your own business, when BAM! You're hit with an avalanche of couples living their best lives. There's Becky and Brad, frolicking on a beach that looks like Bob Ross himself painted it. Meanwhile, you're sitting on your couch, wondering if that mysterious stain on your shirt is mustard or evidence of your last.... wait just a second, I used this in chapter 5, so you know what I mean.

Welcome to the Instagram Hunger Games, where the odds of feeling inadequate are ever in your favour! These filters have more magical powers than Hogwarts. They can turn your average Jono into a Greek god faster than you can say "Valencia." Come on, sing along with

Helmut Lotti – type in your browser the following: https://www.youtube.com/watch?v=-bDWv1NywUE

Valencia
Es la tierra de las flores de la luz y del amor
Valencia
Tus mujeres todas tienen de las rosas el color
Valencia
Al sentir como perfuma en tus huertas el azahar
Quisiera
En la huerta valenciana mis amores encontrar
La blanca barraca, la flor del naranjo
Las huertas floridas, almendros en flor
El Turia de plata, el cielo turquesa
El sol valenciano que van diciendo amor

Suddenly, everyone's skin is smoother than a freshly waxed dolphin, and their teeth are whiter than a suburban mom's Pinterest board.

But here's the kicker, folks: behind every perfect post is a couple who just had a fight about who ate the last slice of Dominos' pizza. That's right, those lovey-dovey pairs with their #couplegoals and #blessed captions? They're just like us mere mortals, except with better lighting and an unhealthy obsession with avocado toast.

Let's be real for a hot second.

Social media is like a highlight reel of people's lives, minus the blooper reel. You don't see posts about "Date night at the ER because Brad thought he could do parkour after three margaritas," or "Romantic getaway ruined because Sally snores like a chainsaw with bronchitis."

Nope, it's all sunsets and soulmates, leaving the rest of us wondering if we missed the memo on how to achieve relationship nirvana.

But fear not, my insecure mates!

For every picture-perfect couple online, there's a real-life duo arguing about whose turn it is to take out the trash or debating the proper way to load a dishwasher or who left the toilet seat up!

That's the good stuff, people!

The real, unfiltered, sometimes-messy-but-always-genuine love that doesn't need a Valencia filter to shine.

So, next time you find yourself spiralling into an Instagram-induced existential crisis, please remember filters can smooth out wrinkles, but they can't filter out relationship farts.

And let's be honest, if your partner still loves you after witnessing your post-burrito fart, that's true #relationshipgoals material right there.

Chapter 8

Maintaining Trust in a World of DMs and Sliding into DMs

Welcome to the wild and wacky world of DMs - the digital equivalent of passing notes in class, except now you're an adult and the teacher can't confiscate your phone!

Once again please buckle up, buttercup, because we're about to dive into the treacherous waters of online flirting, where emojis are the new love letters and trust is as rare as a unicorn riding a rainbow.

For the umpteen time, picture this: You're scrolling through Instagram, minding your own business, when suddenly - BAM! - a message slides into your DMs smoother than a buttered-up penguin on an ice slide. Is it the love of your life?

A Nigerian princess is offering you riches beyond your wildest dreams? Or just another bot trying to sell you protein shakes?

Welcome to the DM roulette, where every message is a mystery and trust is about as stable as a Jenga tower in an earthquake!

Now, let's talk about sliding into DMs.

It's an art form, really.

Some people approach it with the subtlety of a bull in a China shop, while others are so smooth you'd think they bathed in olive oil. But remember, just because someone can craft a witty opening line doesn't mean they're not a serial killer with great grammar. Trust is earned, not given out like free samples at Bunnings during a sausage sizzle sale.

In this digital jungle, catfish are lurking around every corner, ready to pounce on unsuspecting victims with their perfectly crafted fake profiles. That supermodel who just messaged you saying you're the love of their life. Hate to break it to you, but it's just Dave from accounting trying to spice up his sad, lonely life. Trust your gut, mates - if something seems too good to be true, it is.

And let's not forget about the dangers of comparing your life to the carefully curated highlight reels you see on social media.

Sure, @PerfectCouple might look like they're living in a real-life rom-com, but behind those filters and carefully staged photos, they're arguing about whose turn it is to do the dishes.

Remember, Instagram is like the Las Vegas saying - what happens in the filter, stays in the filter.

So how do you maintain trust in this digital wild west?

Well, for starters, don't believe everything you read. That gal claiming to be a one hundred- and fifty-six-centimetres tall neurosurgeon/model/astronaut? Yeah, she's probably Doris at the local Petco and weighs one hundred kilos and is one hundred twenty-eight centimetres tall. Don't be afraid to do a little detective work - Google is your friend, and so is the "video call" button.

Mates, communication is the key!

Be somewhat open, be somewhat honest, and for the love of all that is holy, please use proper punctuation. Nothing says "untrustworthy" like someone who thinks "your" and "you're" are interchangeable.

And if by chance that same gal claiming to be a one 156 centimetres tall neurosurgeon/model/astronaut starts becoming a bit shady or evasive?

Hit that block button faster than you can say "catfish."

Remember, in the world of DMs, trust is like a good Wi-Fi connection - hard to find and easy to lose. So, approach with caution, keep your BS ~~degree~~ detector on high alert, and don't be afraid to call out dishonest behaviour. And if all else fails, just remember there's plenty of fish in the sea... and just as many catfish.

So go forth, my brave digital mates! Navigate those DMs with the caution of a bomb squad technician and the wit of a stand-up comedian. Trust your instincts, verify before you amplify, and always, ALWAYS, think twice before sending that 2 AM "u up?" message. Because in the end, finding true love in the DMs is possible... just about as possible as finding a needle in a haystack while blindfolded and riding a unicycle. But hey, stranger things have happened!

Now, if you'll excuse me, I have a Nigerian princess to respond to. She says her daddy approves me to marry her and all she needs is my is my cheque account number and my mother's maiden name so she can wire me money to fly first class to Nairobi. Seems legit, right?

Chapter 8

The Red Flags of a Catfish

Gather 'round, mates! It's time to dive into the murky waters of online dating, where the catfish swim freely and the profile pictures are as real as a two-sided obverse coin in Australia. I am about to take you on a wild ride through the land of digital deception!

First up, let's talk about those profile pictures that look like they've been ripped straight from the pages of Vogue. If looks are more defined than your life goals and her smile is brighter than your future, it's time to raise an eyebrow higher than her impossibly arched ones. Remember, mates, unless you're swiping in Hollywood, the chances of matching with a supermodel who's "just a simple girl next door" are about as likely as you are winning an Olympic gold medal in underwater basket weaving.

Now, let's address the love bombers - those smooth talkers who shower you with more compliments than a grandmother at a family reunion. If they're telling you you're their soulmate faster than you can say, "what's your last name?", it's time to pump those brakes harder than a L plater. Real love takes time, mates (if that is what you are looking for which to be honest, very few of us are, we are after one thing and one thing only you know what I am talking about I do not need to spell it out for ya!)

Mates, if they're planning your wedding before the first date, they're more interested in your credit card number than your sparkling personality.

Ah, and who could forget the masters of creative writing - those catfish with more plot holes in their backstory than a Michael Bay movie? If their tales are more tangled than your earbuds after a week in your pocket, it's time to channel your inner Sherlock Holmes. Did they grow up in Mosman but somehow have a thick bogan accent? Are they a 25-year-old brain surgeon who also models part time and volunteers at an orphanage for blind puppies? Yeah, and I'm the tooth fairy's personal stylist.

Last but not least, let's talk about that gut feeling (no, not indigestion). Do you know that little voice in your head that whispers "something's fishy" louder than a tuna market at high noon? If your Spidey senses are tingling more than Peter Parker in a bug zapper, it's time to trust that instinct. Your gut has been evolving for millions of years – since the stone age when we used to club them and bring them into our cave. Now it is the other way around.

Women today are smarter than your average catfish and definitely smarter than you. Their entire existence is making your heart drunk for them. Do not become "the one".

So, my dear mates, as you navigate the treacherous seas of online dating, keep these red flags in mind. Be more doubtful than a conspiracy theorist at a Peter Dutton press conference. Ask more questions than a toddler on a sugar high. And for the love of all that is holy, please, PLEASE, don't send money to that Nigerian princess who somehow ended up on Tinder (I did that already and now I am applying at Centrelink for assistance.)

Remember, in the grand game of online dating, you're not just looking to be a catch - you're trying to avoid being caught. So, sharpen those catfish-detecting skills, gents. Be the angler, not the fish. And if all else fails, just remember it's better to be single than to be someone's sucker (unless you have something nice to suck on).

Now go forth, you magnificent, slightly suspicious male creatures! May your matches be real, your conversations be almost genuine, and your dates be catfish-free. And if you do end up falling for a dud, well... at least you'll have a remarkable story for your next mates' night out. Happy fishing!

Chapter 9

The Art of the Profile Picture

The wild world of online dating - where expectations are high, reality is low, and your match's height is as accurate as a weather forecast. Are you tired of showing up to dates feeling like you've been catfished harder than some tuna in the Pacific? I am about to help you dive into the murky waters of profile picture perfection!

First up, let's tackle the infamous bathroom selfie - the photographic equivalent of a participation trophy. Nothing says "I'm a catch" quite like a mirror smudged with toothpaste and a toilet lurking in the background. It's about as appealing as gym socks marinated in vinegar. Trust me, your potential female matches would rather see you posing with a cactus than your collection of half-empty shampoo bottles.

Now, onto the group photo conundrum - or as I like to call it, "Where's Wally: Desperate Singles Edition." Sure, you look like a social butterfly in that snap from your cousin's wedding, but your matches shouldn't need a magnifying glass and the American FBI training to identify you. Save them the headache and stick to solo shots (but not under the sheets doing the nasty). Otherwise, you might as well include a treasure map and a series of cryptic clues in your bio.

Let's not forget the classic "throwback" profile pic. Yes, some mates actually do this photo shot. You know, the one from five years ago when you still had dreams and a metabolism. Newsflash: using an outdated photo is like advertising a Ferrari and showing up in a rusty tricycle. It's time to embrace your current self, dad body and all. Remember, honesty is the best policy (or so the saying goes) but a little photoshopping never hurt if it is done correctly. Just tell them when you meet them that the photo was before the accident in which you save sixteen orphans from the orphanage during an intense fire.

And please, for the love of all that is holy (I keep saying this a lot and I am not even religious), retire those Snapchat filters (yes, although the numbers of users have declined, Snapchat is still incredibly popular). You're not fooling anyone with those dog ears and oversized eyes. Unless you're actually part Chihuahua, in which case, carry on.

Here's a revolutionary idea: how about a picture that actually looks like you? (No, again, a little bit of alteration hurt no one. Think of it as a facelift without the cost).

I know, I know, it's a wild concept. But trust me, it's better to have someone fall for your 'new authentic self' than for the real you. You can work on the details later. Just flash out your Platinum AMEX card and watch them melt in your arms.

Besides, imagine the look on their face when you show up looking exactly like your Photoshop picture. It'll be like seeing a unicorn - rare, magical, and slightly confusing. Disappointment makes them ready for later in life.

In conclusion, mastering the art of the Photoshop profile picture is like making the perfect grilled cheese sandwich - it seems simple, but there's a fine line between golden perfection and a burnt mess. Be almost honest, be almost yourself, and for Pete's sake (whoever he is), keep your bathroom out of it. Remember, you're looking for a nice f**k, not a soulmate. So put your best Photoshop face forward – not your actual face, that is - and dive into the dating pool. Just watch out for the catfish!

Chapter 10

The Truth About Online Dating Deception

The wild and wacky world of online dating - where love blossoms in the glow of smartphone screens and romance is just a swipe away! But beware, dear digital Casanovas, for this virtual playground is rife with more fibs than a politician's campaign speech. Fear not, though! Your trusty guide (Moi!) will take you through the treacherous waters of online deception is here to help you navigate the sea of stretched truths and carefully angled selfies to make you look better than you really are.

You're crafting your online dating profile, and suddenly, you're seized by an overwhelming urge to transform into a taller, younger, more chiselled version of yourself. After all, what's a little white lie between potential ~~sex partners~~, I mean, soulmates, right? Wrong! No RIGHT!!!!

Unless you're planning to show up to your date wearing stilts and a rubber mask, it's best to stick to a somewhat truthful version of the truth. Remember, honesty can get you into trouble but a little white lie, OK, many a lot of little white lies, may get you laid.

Now, let's talk about the fine art of profile pictures. We've all been tempted to use that one photo from five years ago when the lighting was right, and gravity hadn't yet waged its cruel war on our jawlines. But resist overdoing it.

Your potential sack date will wonder if she is really meeting "Indiana Jones" Embrace your current self - wrinkles, dad body, and all (yes I know I repeated myself). Tell them it was a Y2K bug and if they do not know what that means, boy, you got yourself a really young one and better check her driver's license for proof of age. Just say that you are like a fine wine - you only get better with age (and if they don't appreciate that, they can go suck on a grape).

Ah, but what about the dreaded catfish - those slippery characters who slide into your DMs with more fake photos than a tabloid magazine? It works both ways. A beautiful photo of a female may sucker you in and then when you see her, wow, you faint.

These digital deceivers are the chameleons of the online dating world, changing their appearance more often than a mood ring at a therapy session. To avoid falling for their tricks, remember the golden rule of online dating: If they look like a supermodel but claim to be a shy librarian who can't video chat because their webcam is allergic to Tuesdays, it's time to swipe left faster than you can say "catfish and chips."

But fear not, my intrepid mates! There are ways to spot these virtual villains. If their match's profile reads like a badly translated fortune cookie and they declare their undying love faster than you can say "Nigerian princess," it's time to bail quicker than a cat in a bathtub. And if they persistently dodge meetups with excuses more creative than a toddler avoiding bedtime, it's probably time to cast your line elsewhere and check your wallet for your Platinum AMEX might have just been lifted virtually.

Now, let's address the elephant in the chat room (not her) - the temptation to stretch the truth about ourselves too much. Sure, it might be tempting to claim you're a part-time astronaut who moonlights as a gourmet chef, but unless you can whip up a soufflé in zero gravity, it's best to stick to down-to-earth facts but facts that cannot really be confirmed. You do not want to get caught.

Remember, your quirks are what make you unique! So, what if you can't tell the difference between a salad fork and a tuning fork? You are looking for a one-night stand, not a relationship, right?

In the end, almost authenticity is the secret sauce in the recipe for online dating success. Be yourself - your glorious, imperfect, slightly weird self, but do not open those doors too wide and get caught. After all, you're not looking for someone to fall in love with your carefully crafted online persona; you want them to fall in bed and do the NASTY all night long (well, only if you could). Look for some gal that believes that cheese is a food group.

So, my brave mates of the digital dating realm, go forth and be untruthful! Let your freak flag fly higher than a cat video's view count. And remember, in the grand buffet of online dating, it's better to be a genuine creative genius and get laid than a sincere human male whacking himself alone while eating potato chips on the toilet.

Happy swiping!

Chapter 11

Building Trust in a Digital Age

Here you are in the digital age and you are trying to get laid. In today's wild digital jungle, catfishing is like a bad reality show we all accidentally got cast in. Thanks to social media and dating apps, it's easier than ever for people to don fake identities and trick unsuspecting romantics. Imagine fishing, but instead of catching a big, shiny trout, you're left with a soggy boot full of disappointment.

You tried every conceivable way to attract the female, using as many little white lies as possible in a way you do not get caught and then the tables are turned on you.

But worry not, there are ways to navigate this ocean of trickery without getting tangled in their nets. Just as you wouldn't hand over your credit card to a fish (or would you? That's a different problem), it's crucial to swim through the online dating pool with a healthy dose of scepticism. Don't buy every tall tale you hear – always verify before diving in headfirst (unless it is a dive between her legs.)

Social media's impact on dating culture is like a double-edged swordfish. It makes connecting with potential partners as easy as ordering pizza, but it also turns deception into a high-stakes game of hide-and-seek. You are covering your arse to make sure you do not get caught because instead of uncovering hidden treasure, you're a dud but also remember it is a two-way street and not everything that glitters is gold – sometimes it's just a shiny, deceitful twat hiding behind a filter.

Technology's role in modern relationships is like a virtual ball and chain – it can either keep you close to loved ones (your mum, for example) or drag you into the abyss (angry axe wielding husband). It's all about balance, mates. Choose wisely your targets and remember, trust is the glue that holds any relationship together, so avoid it, whether it's through a screen or face-to-face.

So, in this catfish-infested digital age, approach online research for a good one-night stand with caution and a hearty sense of humour. Trust your gut, double-check those stories, and don't shy away from the tough questions (fly away, for these are the ones that will get you in trouble). After all, finding ~~love~~ sex shouldn't feel like a never-ending game of cat and mouse – it should be a genuine connection with someone who values a good nightstand and is willing to walk away without asking you for money.

Mates stay sharp out there, and may your online search bring you sexual escapades that you will never forget (just their names).

Chapter 12

The Rise of Emotional Cheating

Emotional cheating is spreading like a juicy rumour in a high school cafeteria. With just a few clicks, you can find yourself knee-deep in a conversation with someone who isn't worth taking to bed. And let's face it, those heart-eyed emojis are like the gateway drug to Loserville.

It's like we're all starring in a virtual soap opera right in our DMs. One moment you're harmlessly commenting on a meme with the intention of a good one-night stand, and the next, they are spilling their deepest secrets to you, a stranger they just met. Reminds me to install a warming voice like "Danger Will Robinson, danger". Suddenly you're scratching your head and wondering how you got here.

Thanks to social media, connecting with people outside of your range is possible and if you are smart enough, you might just get away with it.

Whether it's sliding into someone's DMs or double tapping every photo they post, the temptation is always lurking. And let's not forget the risk of catfishing – because that hot gal you've been chatting with might just be a 50-year-old hack still living in her mum's basement.

But don't panic, there is a way out of this digital drama. By setting guidelines and monitoring their reactions, you might avoid the hacks and get the ones you want in the sack!

Remember, there is an unfollow button. Use it if she sends you an actual photo, and she is the Wicked Witch of the West.

Finally, resist the urge to send that flirty message to your high school crush, for I am sure her looks have crashed over the years.

So, the next time you're tempted to dabble in a bit of cheating online, remember the golden rule: screw them as fast as you can and move on.

Never give them your phone number and, for goodness' sake, never, ever, send them your actual photo. It makes it easier for the police to track you.

Resist all their love emojis and go forth to the next conquest.

Chapter 13

The Temptation of Sliding into a Stranger's DMs: How to Resist

OK, I have made some rather crude statements in the previous twelve chapters so I feel I must put some redeeming sentences here in other to satisfy those readers who spent money on this paperback or eBook (no audiobook, for no decent voice actor would touch it).

So, if you are tired of scrolling through your social media feed and feeling like everyone else has found love (or sex) except for you? Do you find yourself tempted to slide into a stranger's DMs in the hopes of finding your own fairytale ending (in the sack, of course)? Well, before you hit send on that risky message, let's talk about how to resist the temptation of sliding into a stranger's DMs in the digital dating world.

First and foremost, remember that just because someone looks good on social media doesn't mean they're the right sexual match for you. It's easy to get caught up in the perfectly curated photos and witty captions, but the reality is often far from what you see online. So, resist the urge to reach out to someone based solely on their online persona – you never know what's lurking behind those Instagram filters.

Second, consider the potential consequences of sliding into a stranger's DMs. While it may seem harmless to shoot your shot with a witty message or flirty emoji (your penis covered in flowers), you never know how the other person will respond. They could be in a committed relationship (can be bad for scoring), not interested in having sex with a male (maybe they like the same sex), or even worse – a catfish looking to deceive unsuspecting souls. So, before you hit send, think about whether it's worth the risk of potentially embarrassing yourself or getting entangled in a messy situation.

Next, focus on building genuine connections with people in real life tell you about their pathetic life and could be an easy score. Rather than relying on social media as your sole source of romantic prospects, hit a bar or pub where older women gather, you might get lucky, for they have money and can be incredibly grateful if you service them.

While it's fun to swipe through dating apps or scroll through Instagram looking for potential sexual matches, nothing beats the thrill of meeting someone in person, squeezing their boobs or arse and seeing their reaction.

If you do not get slapped or the police are called, baby, what a night you have in store for yourself.

Resist the temptation to hide behind your screen and instead, put yourself out there in the real world – you never know where you might find sex.

Remember that there's no rush to find sex online. Women are desperate to find 'Mr Right', just pretend you are him.

Resist the urge to rush into a sexual romp with someone you barely know just for the sake of having a good time – focus on what she is after and if it means she wants to build a strong foundation of trust and connection with you then run brother, run.

In conclusion, while the temptation to slide into a stranger's DMs may be strong, it's important to resist the urge and approach digital sexual encounters with caution and a healthy dose of scepticism. Trust me, your future self will thank you for it.

PS – I hope this satisfies the need for *'redeeming values in this book'* people.

Chapter 14

Rebuilding Trust After a Social Media Infidelity

Let's talk about the role of technology in modern relationships. Forget passing notes in class or sending love letters through snail mail – those days are as dead as dial-up internet. Now, we're all about instant communication, constant notifications, and emojis galore. But remember, with great Wi-Fi comes great responsibility – use your tech skills for finding good sex, not for commitments.

Ah, social media, and infidelity – a tale as old as Facebook (or at least MySpace). Whether it's a cheeky DM or a full-blown online affair, digital cheating can blow up your love life faster than a viral TikTok. But don't worry, trust can be rebuilt with time, effort, and a truckload of white lies.

Catfishing and online dating deception might sound like MTV's reality show drama, but it's more common than you'd think. So, remember before she swipes right on that profile you made up which seems straight out of a rom-com, she might just channel her inner Sherlock Holmes and, with a little sleuthing, can see you right through.

In conclusion, keeping trust alive in the digital age might feel like climbing Everest in flip-flops, but with humour, and your wallet filled with bills, you can conquer even the toughest challenges of any lawyer she hired to get you jailed. Remember, social media is just a tool – it's up to you to use it wisely. So go forth, my fellow males, and may your digital dating adventures be filled with laughter, sex, and a hefty supply of condoms.

Chapter 15

The Realities of Cyber Cheating and How to Protect Your Relationship

With a chapter title like the one above, you would expect a serious tone and a decent chapter on relationships, but you really missed the point of the book and this chapter. It is about protection and what protects a man: a condom.

Ah, the condom – that trusty little rubber companion standing guard at the gates of unplanned parenthood and pesky STIs. But what exactly makes a condom a "safe" condom? Let's unravel this latex mystery with a touch of humour.

First off, size matters – and we're not just talking about what's in the pants. A safe condom is one that fits like a glove. Too tight, and it's a recipe for disaster. Too loose, and, well, it's like throwing a hot dog down a hallway. Find the Goldilocks of condoms: not too tight, not too loose, but exactly right.

Next up, check the expiration date. Yes, condoms have a shelf life! Using an expired condom is like trusting a rusty old parachute – it might work, but do you really want to take that risk? Always check the date and ensure you're not gambling with ancient latex.

Material is key too. Latex is the old standby, but for those allergic to it, there are alternatives like polyurethane or polyisoprene. Think of it as choosing between different flavours of ice cream – just pick the one that doesn't give you hives.

And finally, store it properly. A condom left in a hot car is about as useful as a chocolate teapot. Keep them cool and dry, away from sharp objects. After all, a condom is only as good as its integrity – and its ability to withstand the heat, both literally and metaphorically.

In conclusion, a safe condom is one that fits well, isn't expired, suits your material preference, and is stored properly. Now, go forth and prosper, armed knowing that your condom game is on point!

Chapter 16

The Pros and Cons of Maintaining a Long-Distance Relationship Online

Ah, the long-distance sexual conquest – where interest spans miles, and patience stretches thinner than cheap toilet paper. What exactly makes a long-distance relationship a pain? Let's dive into this romantic torture and hope we find some answers we can use.

First up, time zones. Nothing screams phone sex or online sex like a 3 AM video call. Your new sexual partner's whispering sweet nothings while you're fighting to stay awake, looking like a zombie auditioning for a horror flick. Coordinating schedules feels like planning an international summit.

Next, the eternal buffering. That moment when you're ready to explode, and the screen freezes mid-sentence. You're left staring at a pixelated face, wondering if they're contemplating your love stick or just stuck in internet limbo.

Don't forget the travel costs. Should be able to really get into it with her and want to go for the 'real thing', seeing her in person would be a precious treat – and your bank account's worst nightmare. Plane tickets and petrol money all add up. Your wallet cries a little every time you book another flight.

Luckily, when using online sex or phone sex, there is no need to show genuine affection and you can become a pro at sending kiss emojis and virtual hugs, so milk them as much as possible.

In summary, long-distance relationships are a test of your patience and Wi-Fi connections. They're filled with time zone woes, buffering, potential costly travel plans (if you are brave enough), and emoji overuse. But if you can wack yourself every night, maybe, just maybe, it's all worth it.

Chapter 17

Virtual Date Night

What makes these digital rendezvous so great for spicing things up? Let's dive into the saucy side of virtual dating with a humorous twist.

First, there's the anticipation. Nothing says "I'm into you" enjoy spending an hour setting up your laptop, adjusting lighting, and finding that perfect angle. Your penis must look good, always. It's like prepping for a Hollywood movie, except the only critic is your date, and the genre is steamy sex.

Next, the attire. From the waist up, you're dressed in nothing! No need to impress – you both know what is going to happen. Below the waist? Well, I am sure you know that answer.

Now, in her case, she will be wearing something. Something in the ultimate comfort-meets-sexy combo, where she feels both seductive and snuggly. But you really do not care as long as it comes off in the first twenty seconds after saying "Hi."

Then there's the creative foreplay. Goodness, I am laughing at this last sentence. What creative foreplay. Your mind has been rasing a million kilometres an hour, so you are ready. All you got to do is to aim and fire!

But wait she might need for you to send her a few flirty texts, seductive emojis, and suggestive GIFs to set the scene, you know, get her in the mood.

By the time you're face-to-face on the screen, the sexual tension is thicker than a plot twist in a Telenovela, but you might have already finished, let's hope not, because she has not even started.

If you have not finished (look down at your boy and thank him) now you can explore new realms of role-playing with fun filters – ever wanted to seduce as a pirate or a cute puppy? Now's your chance.

Finishing the Virtual sex nights also eliminates the awkward post-escape. No need to sneak out or call an Uber – just hit "End Call" and you're back in your own space. It's a clean getaway with none of the morning-after logistics.

So virtual sex nights blend anticipation, comfy attire (for her – none for you), creative foreplay (again, for her), and an easy withdrawal plan to create a uniquely exciting and hassle-free experience. So, fire up that webcam, dim the lights, and let the digital sparks fly!

Chapter 18

The Challenges of Trust and Communication in a Long-Distance Relationship

One more thing I need to tell you about is the challenge of trust in a long-distance sexual relationship.

Building trust in a virtual sex relationship – now there's a digital tightrope act worthy of Cirque du Soleil. Let's explore what it takes to trust someone you've never actually met, all the while keeping it straight to the point: ejaculation.

First, there's the identity verification. It's 2024 – no one wants to find out they've been sexting a chatbot. A quick video call can confirm that the person sending those steamy messages isn't a rogue AI. Nothing builds trust, like knowing your partner has a pulse and isn't a Terminator in disguise or a police officer.

Next, we have the art of encryption. Trust means knowing your intimate conversations won't end up on Reddit's front page. Secure apps with end-to-end encryption are your best friends. After all, no one wants their virtual escapades turning into a public spectacle. What would your mother say?

Then, there's the mutual respect of boundaries. You've got to trust that your sex partner won't screenshot or record your tiny willy and spread it on the web. It's like the unspoken rule of the virtual bedroom: what happens in the chat stays in the chat.

Communication is key, but in a virtual sex relationship, it's on steroids. Clear discussions about desires, limits, and expectations are vital. It's all about that sexy combo of vulnerability and transparency, without the risk of awkward eye contact.

And let's not forget good grammar – the secret ingredient that keeps things from getting too serious. Sharing a laugh over a typo or a quirky autocorrect can turn a potentially awkward moment into a trust-building experience. Because nothing says "I trust you" like laughing together at an accidentally sent eggplant emoji up your butt hole. In conclusion, trust in a virtual sex relationship is built on verified identities (even if they are not real), encrypted apps, stellar communication, and plenty of lubricants to facilitate her and you. Keep it secure, and you might just find that virtual sex gives you no STD at all!

Chapter 19

Navigating Time Zones and Technology Hiccups in a Long-Distance Relationship

I already spoke about this in the previous chapter, so I will repeat nothing here.

This page contains a link you can use to schedule your sexual escapades accordingly.

Enjoy yourself.

https://www.timeanddate.com/worldclock/converter.html?iso=20161226T000000&p1=240&p2=25

Chapter 20

Online Dating Etiquette: How to Make a Good First Impression

Listen up, lovelorn ~~leeches~~ lotharios in distress! Navigating the treacherous waters of online dating can be trickier than trying to eat soup with a fork. But fear not, for I shall bestow upon you the sacred wisdom of not making a complete fool of yourself in the virtual realm of online conquest..

First things first (and I know I am repeating myself), resist the urge to use that blurry selfie where you look like a constipated chipmunk. Instead, opt for a photo that actually comes close to resembling you – shocking concept, so if you pick a photo of Chris Hemsworth and you do not come close, then if asked, just say that the accident was not your fault.

When crafting your profile, avoid the clichés, like "looking for my kinky soulmate" or "fluent in sexy talk." We get it, you're unique – just like everyone else.

Now, when messaging your potential future ex, remember the golden rule: don't be too creepy. Resist the temptation to open with "Hey baby, you like it doggy style?" or "I've already got the protection, let's get down!" Instead, try something revolutionary, like actually reading their profile and working that into the conversation in a way that gets you laid. Now, that is thoughtful.

Oh, and for the love of all that is holy, proofread your messages. Nothing says, "I'm a catch" quite like confusing "your" and "you're" or declaring your undying need for sex by saying "Hey, want to see my angel" but meaning "Hey, want to see my dangle."

Follow these tips, and you'll be well on your way to impressing that special someone – or at least not getting blocked within the first five minutes.

Chapter 21

The Golden Rule of Digital Dating: Treat Others How You Want to Be Treated

I believe that online dating is like the wild west,. It is where etiquette goes to die, and social skills are optional! Want to make a lasting impression? Let me tell you how to make it a disaster.

First off, forget everything you've learned about respect and common decency. That's so last century! Instead, embrace the chaos. Start by crafting a profile pic that screams "I'm definitely not a serial killer" - think dimly lit bathroom selfies or grainy shots of you chugging beer at your cousin's wedding giving the bride the tongue.

When it comes to your bio, less is more. And by less, we mean zero effort. "DTF" (Da Total F**k) is a perfectly acceptable entire profile. Bonus points if you can misspell it.

Now, for messaging. Remember, persistence is key. If they don't respond to your first "hey," send it again. And again. And again. Nothing says "I'm interested" quite like borderline harassment.

I think I am a writer so I will keep repeating this: Grammar? Spelling? Punctuation? Pfft! Who needs 'em? Real attraction is built on deciphering "u up?" at 2 AM.

Lastly, if you do score a sex date, make sure to arrive late, talk only about yourself, and definitely check your phone every two minutes. After all, you're a catch, and they should feel lucky to be in your presence.

Follow these tips, and you'll continue to be single for a long time! Congratulations, you've mastered the art of treating others how you absolutely do not want to be treated.

Happy swiping!

Chapter 22

Avoiding Oversharing: Keeping Things Private in a Digital Relationship

Welcome, digital sexbirds, to the fine art of keeping your virtual sexcapades mysterious! In a world where sharing is caring, we're here to tell you that oversharing is scaring. It's time to learn how to keep your digital drawbridge raised and your emotional moat full.

First rule of the Tight-Lipped Club: Don't talk about Tight-Lipped Club. Or your childhood trauma. Or your ex. Or that weird rash. Remember, mystery is sexy; your detailed sexual exploits, however, are not. Here I support the saying: "Sharing is caring."

When crafting messages, channel your inner Magic 8-Ball. Keep 'em vague and open to interpretation. "Cannot predict now" is a perfectly acceptable response to "What are you doing this weekend?"

Resist the urge to live-tweet your potential sex partner moans while you are doing the fandango. Your followers don't need a play-by-play of your doodle doing its job. And do not even think of putting your penis on a pizza and saying: "Eat up, babe. It's a sausage pizza!" and send out a photo with the note "Oh, food pics!"

Sharing passwords? Ha! Good one. Your Netflix account is your fortress. Guard it like a dragon guards gold.

Remember, a little intrigue goes a long way. Let them wonder about your job (if you have one), your hobbies (porn), and whether you're actually a secret agent. (Spoiler: You're not, but they don't need to know that.)

In conclusion, keep 'em guessing, keep 'em interested, and keep your therapist on speed dial.

Happy (un) sharing!

Chapter 23

The Importance of Setting Boundaries in a Digital Relationship

Did I not cover this already in a previous chapter? Well, just in case, let me refresh your little grey cells. Imagine you're diving headfirst into a virtual playground where everyone is as stunning as a supermodel and as charming as a stand-up comedian (excuse I think I am going to vomit. I will be right back).

OK, let's continue. In this world (that does not exist), your avatar can woo anyone with the flick of a pixelated eyebrow. But wait! Before you unleash your inner sexual Casanova, let's talk about why, even in a digital sex romp, you even need to have boundaries.

First off, virtual consent is as real as your Wi-Fi bill. Just because you're behind a screen doesn't mean you can behave like a wild chimpanzee at a banana buffet. Respect your fellow avatars; they have feelings too, even if they're represented by a 3D-rendered fox or a neon-coloured elf.

Allow them to show their 'stuff' first and then you show yours. It is a reasonable request.

Next, consider the virtual STDs – "Sparkly Tits Disorder." Add these additional moments such as awkwardness, digital ghosting, and the dreaded "Did I just hit on my banana?" scenario. Boundaries help you avoid these pixelated pitfalls.

Lastly, think about the chaos of a boundary-less digital world. It'd be like letting toddlers loose in a candy store with no supervision – amusing for a second, then absolute pandemonium.

So, while it's tempting to let your avatar run wild and free, remember that boundaries keep the digital playground fun and drama-free. And trust me, nobody wants a virtual slap on the wrist or a permanent ban from the coolest online hangout.

Chapter 24

#RelationshipGoals vs. Reality: The Truth Behind the Perfect Instagram Couple

As I near the end of the book, I am reminded that some social redemption chapters need to be included, so I will try my best in this one to give the reader some good advice. Let's start.

In the age of Instagram filters and perfectly curated feeds, it's easy to fall into the trap of comparing our own ~~penis~~ relationships with those of the seemingly flawless couples we see online. But let's face it, behind every #RelationshipGoals post lies a reality that is far from perfect. Before you start feeling down about your own ~~ding dong~~ love life, remember that what you see on social media is often a carefully crafted facade.

We've all seen those couples who seem to have it all together on Instagram - ~~the matching dildoes~~, the matching outfits, the romantic vacations, the perfectly staged photos. But let's be real, nobody's relationship is as picture-perfect as it appears online. In reality, most couples argue over who forgot to ~~put on the condom~~, put out the trash or whether to watch Netflix or ~~'Debbie does the Dallas cheerleaders'~~ or Hulu. So next time you find yourself feeling envious of a couple's online presence, just remember that they're arguing about something trivial behind the scenes.

Social media has a way of distorting our perceptions of reality, especially when it comes to relationships. It's easy to get caught up in the comparison game and start doubting the strength of your own relationship. But the truth is, no relationship is without its flaws and imperfections. So instead of striving for an unattainable standard of perfection, focus on building a sound foundation of trust, communication, and mutual respect for your partner.

The intersection of social media and infidelity is a slippery slope that many couples have to navigate in today's digital age. With the temptation of reconnecting with old flames or engaging in online flirtations, it's more important than ever to set boundaries and establish trust in your relationship. Remember, what you do online can have real-life consequences, so think twice before sliding into someone's DMs or liking an ex's post. (God, this paragraph was so boring!!!!!!)

At the end of the day, the portrayal of relationships on social media is just that - a portrayal. Don't let the curated feeds and filtered photos fool you into thinking that anyone's love life is perfect. Instead, focus on building a strong, healthy ~~penis~~ relationship with open communication, trust, and respect. And remember, a little humour and humility can go a long way in navigating the ups and downs of modern ~~sexual acts~~ dating in the digital age.

Chapter 25

The Pressure to Perform: How Social Media Influences Relationship Expectations

Adjust your leather harnesses and adjust your fuzzy handcuffs, because we're diving into the wild world of kinky performance anxiety!

Picture this: You're trying to be the Christian Grey of your dreams, but you're more "Fifty Shades of Beige." You've got the whip, you've got the chains, but you've also got the coordination of a drunk octopus trying to put on roller skates.

Suddenly, you're expected to transform from mild-mannered accountant Bob into "Lord Dominicus, Conqueror of Consensual Chaos." But let's be real, the only thing you've ever dominated is a spreadsheet.

You've watched all the tutorials, but tying elaborate knots in the heat of the moment is harder than it looks. Your partner's expecting a Gordian Knot, but you're serving up something that looks like a cat got into the yarn basket.

And don't even get started on the roleplay. You're supposed to be a fierce Viking warrior, but you sound more like a confused tourist asking for directions to the nearest IKEA.

Remember, kinksters: it's okay if your "dungeon" is just your basement with some mood lighting. Rome wasn't built in a day, and neither was your leather daddy persona. Keep practicing, and maybe someday you'll graduate from "Fifty Shades of Beige" to at least "Fifty Shades of Taupe."

Chapter 26

Embracing Imperfection: Finding Love Beyond the Filters and Façade

Alright, you perfectly imperfect perverts, let's talk about getting down and dirty in the real world! Forget those airbrushed fantasies – we're diving into the messy, awkward, hilarious reality of sex with actual human beings.

Picture this: You're finally naked with your dream sex partner, and suddenly you realise your "six-pack" is more of a "party keg." But fear not! Your love handles just mean there's more of you to love (and grab onto during those wild moments).

Some of your ladies might try doing a seductive strip tease only to get tangled in their own bra. "Congratulations, you've just invented a new dance move!" you tell her, so she does not lose the "mood".

Mates, when your "little soldier" decides to take an unexpected nap, just remember – it's not performance anxiety, just tell her it's just a "tactical resting."

Let's not forget the symphony of bodily sounds that accompany our carnal orchestra. That wasn't a fart, it was a "love trumpet." And those squeaky bedsprings? That's just your mattress cheering you on!

Remember, in the realm of real-life romping, perfection is overrated. Embrace and celebrate the beautiful mess that is human intimacy. After all, it's not about being perfect – it's about finding the perfect imperfections together.

Chapter 27

Celebrating Real Love: Navigating the Ups and Downs of a Relationship in the Digital Age

The age-old question that's puzzled philosophers, sexperts, and confused university students since time immemorial: "Was that real sex?" Buckle up, buttercup, we're about to embark on a journey through the murky waters of sexual definition!

Once again, picture this: you've just had an encounter that left you more confused than a chameleon in a bag of Skittles. Was it sex? Was it heavy petting? Was it an elaborate handshake gone horribly wrong? Who knows!

Did clothes come off? Or did you just strategically rearrange them like a game of sexy Tetris? Did things get hot and heavy, or just lukewarm and slightly damp? Was there penetration, or just an enthusiastic game of "Just the Tip"?

Maybe you're wondering if it counts if it lasted shorter than your average TikTok video. Or if it still qualifies when you spent more time trying to open the condom wrapper than actually doing the deed.

Remember, mates, "real sex" is like art - hard to define, but you know it when you see it (or do it). To paraphrase the America pastime, was it a home run, or did you barely make it to first base? The important thing is: Did you have fun? Did you consent? And most importantly, did you remember where you left your underwear?

Chapter 28

Sexting: From Flirty Messages to Explicit Photos

Alright, you digital sex fiends, are you ready for a wild ride through the tantalizing world of sexting? We're talking thumb-cramping action from innocent winky faces to full-frontal selfies that would make your grandma faint.

It all starts innocently enough. A cheeky "u up?" at 2 AM. Before you know it, you're engaged in a high-stakes game of innuendo tennis, lobbing double entendres (not sure what this word means, but it looks intelligent) back and forth like verbal foreplay ninjas.

But wait!

Suddenly, things escalate faster than a caffeinated chipmunk on a rocket. Your witty wordplay morphs into descriptions so steamy they could fog up your screen. You're basically writing erotic literature with one thumb while trying not to drop your phone on your face (you know what is happening now, or do I need to spell it out?).

Then comes the photo request. Panic! Do you risk it? Is that lighting flattering? Is that angle of your dangle hiding your "quarantine 15"? And make sure there's nothing embarrassing in the background like your teddy bear!

Remember, sext-perts, once you hit send, there's no take-backsies. That photo is out there faster than you can say "Oh no, wrong chat!" So maybe think twice before you turn your phone into a pocket-sized peep show.

Happy sexting and may your autocorrect always be in your favour!

Chapter 29

Virtual Reality: Taking Cybersex to a Whole New Level

Prepare to jack in (pun intended) to the wild world of VR hanky-panky. We're talking cybersex so real, you'll forget you're actually alone in your room, flailing around like an inflatable tube man at a car dealership.

Now you do not even need another person!

Gone are the days of AOL chatrooms (yes, I just dated myself to any American reader) and pixelated webcams. Now, you can strap on your headset (and anything else you want) and dive headfirst into a 3D wonderland of polygonal pleasure. It's like "The Matrix," but instead of dodging bullets, you're dodging... well, use your imagination.

You're on a virtual date, trying to look cool in your digital avatar. Suddenly, you realise you forgot to design your virtual pants. Oops! At least in VR, you can blame it on a glitch.

But beware! VR sexcapades come with their own unique hazards. Nothing kills the mood quite like accidentally punching your real-life lamp while reaching for your virtual partner. And let's not forget the potential for some seriously awkward moments if your mother walks in on your mid-session.

Remember, what happens in VR, stays in VR... unless you forgot to close your Twitch stream. Strap in, power up, and get ready for some seriously immersive intimacy.

Just don't forget to hydrate in the real world!

Chapter 30

The Role of Social Media in Breakups and Makeups

The rollercoaster of romantic entanglements! We're diving into the world of breakups and makeups faster than you can say, "It's not you, it's me."

One minute you're riding high on cloud sixty-nine, the next you're sobbing into a six-pack of beer, wondering how it all went wrong. Was it the way you chewed her little twat? Your questionable taste in reality TV? Or perhaps your tendency to narrate your own life in the third person?

Then comes the makeup. Suddenly, all is forgiven because they looked fantastic in that Instagram story that you photoshopped. You're back together faster than you can block and unblock their number. It's like relationship whiplash, but with more dramatic text messages.

And let's not forget the "break" – that magical period where you're technically single but still stalking their social media like it's your full-time job. Are they really "just sex friends" with that gym selfie enthusiast?

Remember, dear male readers, in the game of sexual conquest, sometimes you win, sometimes you lose, and sometimes you end up in a situationship so complicated it would make a soap opera writer's head spin.

Here's to the breakups that strengthen us, the makeups that keep us on our toes, and the next six-pack of beer that gets us through it all!

Chapter 31

The Pressure to Define the Relationship: Are We Exclusive?

Now we come to an unusual, odd question of digital fidelity! Welcome to the brave new world where your relationship status is more complicated than a quantum physics equation.

You're in a torrid affair with someone you've never met in person. You've seen more of their pixels than their pores, and your most intimate moments involve a strong Wi-Fi connection. Then she asks you: are we exclusive? Cue the existential crisis!

Are you cheating if you slide into another DM? Is it two-timing if you have a steamy session in Second Life while your main squeeze is offline? These are the questions that keep virtual us males up at night (or maybe that's just the blue light from their screens).

You might be thinking, "We've never even held hands in real life! Surely I can swipe right on Tinder?" But beware!

Your digital darling might consider your Snapchat streak with that cute coworker as the ultimate betrayal.

Remember, in the world of online sexual escapades, exclusivity is about as clear as dial-up modem sounds. Are you exclusive? Maybe. Are you confused? Definitely. Is it time for an awkward conversation via emoji-laden text?

Absolutely.

Welcome to modern romance, where your relationship status is always "It's complicated" – even in binary.

Chapter 32

Emojis and GIFs: The New Language of Love

I will be addressing this chapter to both the male readers and the occasional female reader, so I try to be extra clean. Here it goes.

Ladies and gentlemen, welcome to the digital age of seduction, where your ability to woo is directly proportional to your emoji game! Gone are the days of flowery sonnets and love letters - now it's all about that strategically placed eggplant or peach.

You're trying to set the mood, and instead of whispering sweet nothings to each other, you're furiously scrolling through your GIF keyboard. Nothing says "I'm in the mood" quite like a gyrating Michael Jackson, right?

But beware! One wrong emoji can turn your sexcapade into a comedy of errors. Send a instead of a and suddenly your steamy chat becomes a Taco Tuesday invitation.

And let's' not forget the art of GIF foreplay. Is that "come hither look" from Emma Stone setting the right tone, or did you just inadvertently friend zone yourself?

Remember, in this brave new world, your flirting skills are only as good as your internet connection.

So, whether you're an emoji virtuoso or a GIF greenhorn, remember in the game of digital sex escapades, he/she who hesitates to send that Winky face is lost.

Now go forth and let your 🍆 and 🍑 fly!

Chapter 33

Misinterpreting Tone in Online Conversations

In the digital dance of miscommunication, where does tone go to die and how does sarcasm get lost in the void of cyberspace? But fear not, intrepid internet sex-interactors, for in this chaos lies an opportunity!

You attempt to send a flirty message, but it's' received as a declaration of war. Oops! But wait - now you are mysterious and unpredictable. Lean into it! Always compare potential sex dates to battle strategies. Isn't that normal?

Perhaps your witty banter is taken as stone-cold seriousness. Suddenly, you are just so funny; you are an intellectual powerhouse! You would make statements like: "I always ponder the socioeconomic implications of a ~~penis~~ pineapple pizza."

Unintentionally, you come across as overly enthusiastic about your panty collection. Congratulations, you just became the most interesting person they have ever met!

The key is to roll with the punches. Typed "You hot" but autocorrect changed it to "You s**t" Now you are an arsehole and there goes your chances of getting laid.

Remember, in the world of online communication, it's not about what you say, it's about how creative you can backpedal when it's misunderstood.

Happy misinterpreting!

Chapter 34

The Impact of Social Media on Marriage and Commitment

Let's take a moment to discuss the above chapter title somewhat seriously because these are the treacherous waters of social media and its impact on matrimony!

You're happily married, poorly content with your partner's sexual antics and questionable fashion choices. Then BAM! Social media enters stage left, and suddenly you're faced with a parade of seemingly perfect potential new sexual partners and maybe even the one who got away from you in high school or university. Your current partner's high school sweetheart is now a yoga instructor with abs you could grate cheese on and you, well, the American Pillsbury doughboy looks better than you. Fantastic.

Let's not forget the joy of passive-aggressive statuses. Nothing says "I desire you" quite like airing your dirty laundry for all 500 of your closest "friends" to see by a slip up of a keystroke.

"Someone forgot to take out the trash again," - Subtlety? Never heard of her.

And oh, the temptation of the DM slide! Your partner's old flame just happened to like that decade-old beach photo. Innocent? Perhaps. Anxiety-inducing? Absolutely.

Remember, mates, in the world of likes, shares, and story views, your attention is now measured in joint profile pictures and cheesy anniversary posts. #BlessedButStressed So, here's to navigating the minefield of social media without blowing up your good thing that you got going.

May your boner be stronger than your Wi-Fi signal!

Chapter 35

Finding Love in the Digital Age: Is It Still Possible?

You know, the eternal quest for a decent romp in the era of swipe-right romance can be stressful. Again, let me try to guide you through the shaky waters of digital desire.

Remember the good old days when finding a sex partner meant making awkward eye contact across a smoky bar? Now it's all about crafting the perfect profile pic that says, "I'm sexy, but not trying too hard" (spoiler: you're totally trying too hard).

You swipe through an endless parade of fish pics and gym selfies, wondering if you'll ever find someone who doesn't think "DTF" is an acceptable opener. Is it too much to ask for someone who can spell "definitely" correctly and doesn't list "fluent in sarcasm" as a personality trait?

But wait! You match with someone who seems perfect. They're witty, attractive, and actually read your made-up bio and believe it! You arrange to meet (only recommended if you get to squeeze her Norks!, refer to chapter 13, but you go anyway), heart pounding with anticipation. Will they look like their photos? Will there be sexual chemistry? Or will you end up with another story for your "worst sex chance to ever have sex with another being from this planet" collection?

Is finding a suitable sex partner still possible in the digital age? Well, it's like panning for gold in a river of eggplant emojis - challenging, but not impossible.

Happy hunting, you sexy, horny keyboard warriors!

Chapter 36

Conclusions to Ponder

As we say goodbye to the wild world of social media, where your every move is broadcasted to the masses faster than you can say "privacy settings." In this concluding chapter, I will recap in a serious manner the delicate dance of balancing privacy and sharing in a world where oversharing has become the norm.

Let's face it - we live in a world where everyone and their grandma (literally) have a social media account. From Facebook to Instagram to TikTok, we're constantly bombarded with photos, updates, and TMI posts from our friends, stalkers, exes, family, and that one person from high school you haven't spoken to in years. It can be overwhelming trying to keep up with all the latest gossip and drama, but hey, it's all part of the fun, right?

But here's the thing - with great power comes great responsibility. Just because you can share every detail of your life with the world doesn't mean you should. It's important to strike a balance between sharing the highlights of your life and keeping some things private.

After all, do we really need to know about your latest bathroom selfie or your play-by-play of last night's date? Probably not.

So how do you navigate this tricky terrain? One word: boundaries. Set clear boundaries for yourself and stick to them. Think twice before hitting that "post" button and ask yourself, "Is this something I want the entire world to see?" If the answer is no, then maybe it's best to keep it to yourself.

At the end of the day, social media is a tool for connection and communication, but it shouldn't come at the expense of your privacy. So go ahead, share those funny memes and cute cat videos, but remember to keep a little mystery for yourself. After all, a little privacy hurt no one - except maybe that one person from high school who still hasn't figured out how to respect boundaries.

As you have read, I was dead serious in this ending chapter. I hope you got a few smiles, maybe a laugh or two and only grimace a few times and, swallowed, tolerated my crude statements.

Here is to your happy sex life!

Questions?

Email me at sex@jfnodar.com.au

José F. Nodar

Flung into one of life's biggest challenges at just eleven, José's story began in Havana, Cuba. The Cuban revolution forced him onto a plane alone, landing him at an orphanage in a small Georgia town called Washington. Reuniting with his parents wouldn't happen until he was eighteen, a high school graduate in Atlanta.

Business Administration became his focus at Georgia State University. From there, he navigated the world of finance, first at the First National Bank of Atlanta (now Wells Fargo) and later as a project manager in financial consulting. These roles took him across the United States, Europe, and even Australia.

It was in Camden, New South Wales, Australia, that a spark ignited José's creative side. A writers' group became the launching pad for his debut novel, and soon, his mind birthed Danny Monk, his first major character.

Currently, José is a prolific writer, working on his seventh short story collection alongside a new crime novel slated for release in 2025.

But José's life isn't all about writing. When he's ~~not having sex~~ crafting captivating stories, you might find him at the local mall, observing the world and gathering inspiration for future characters. Away from his computer, he dives into books or enjoys long, leisurely walks with his wife Miriam around Camden.

www.ingramcontent.com/pod-product-compliance
Lightning Source LLC
Chambersburg PA
CBHW061108100726
47911CB00012B/452